KING COO

The CURSE of the MUMMY'S GOLD

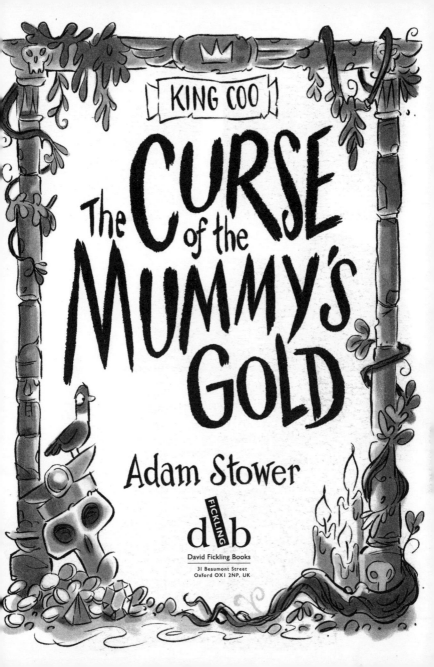

KING COO

The CURSE of the MUMMY'S GOLD

Adam Stower

dlb

David Fickling Books

31 Beaumont Street
Oxford OX1 2NP, UK

Also by Adam Stower:

King Coo

King Coo – The Curse of the Mummy's Gold
is a
DAVID FICKLING BOOK

First published in Great Britain in 2019 by
David Fickling Books,
31 Beaumont Street,
Oxford, OX1 2NP

Text and Illustrations © Adam Stower

978-1-788450-52-2

1 3 5 7 9 10 8 6 4 2

Papers used by David Fickling Books are from well-
managed forests and other responsible sources.

MIX
Paper from
responsible sources
FSC® C018072

DAVID FICKLING BOOKS Reg. No. 8340307

A CIP catalogue record for this book is available from the British Library.

Typeset in 12.5/19pt Goudy Old Style by Falcon Oast Graphic Art Ltd.
Printed and bound in Great Britain by Clays Ltd, Elcograf S.p.A.

For Matt

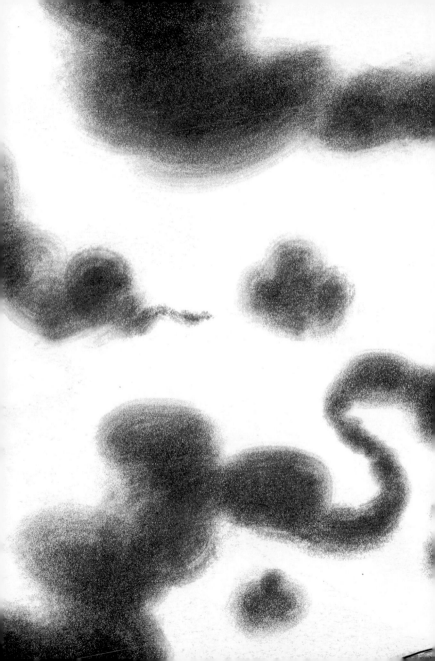

CHAPTER ONE

I f there's one thing that is sure to get a boy out of a warm bed on a chilly morning, it's the smell of smoke.

Sniff...

Blink Blink

Ben shrieked, jolting wide awake. 'Mum! Dad! FIRE! FIIIRE!'

He leaped out of bed and hurled himself down the stairs with all the grace of a donkey on skates.

Thick smoke curled from the kitchen. Ben took a deep breath and burst through the door.

'Dad?' Ben coughed, peering through the plumes of smoke that billowed from the frying pan in Mr Pole's hand. 'What's going on?'

'I'm on breakfast duty.' Mr Pole beamed proudly. 'Mum starts her new job today. At the museum, remember?'

Ben wiped the tears from his stinging eyes and flinched as another sausage exploded and burst into flames.

'Oh dear, crack open a window will you, Ben?' said Mrs Pole emerging through the fug. She kissed Mr Pole on the cheek and cast a wary eye over the sausages rattling around in the pan. 'Just cereal for me I think, thanks love. I don't want to be late.'

'All the more bangers for us, eh, Ben?' said Mr Pole enthusiastically. 'But perhaps you'd best pop on some clothes, eh?' he chuckled, looking Ben up and down. 'Aren't you a bit old to be running round in nothing but your under-grumblies?'

Ben got dressed and was back at the kitchen table just as his dad was dishing up breakfast.

'I like your uniform, Mum,' said Ben, tapping his sausage with the edge of a knife, trying to find a soft spot.

'Thanks, love,' said Mrs Pole, giving her gold badge a little polish with her napkin. 'It's not bad, is it? Oh dear, hold on, listen to this,' she said, turning up the volume on the radio. 'It sounds like there's been another burglary!'

'...The Midnight Mob has struck again! In the third daring raid in as many weeks, a hoard of gold coins has been stolen from the Viking Museum in the town of Bumbleton. There are still no clues as to the identities of the gang responsible. And in other news a fat badger has been found wedged in the water flume at the City pool...'

'Bumbleton?' said Ben. 'That's quite near, isn't it?'

'Yup!' said Mr Pole, who was busy trying to cut his sausage in half with a bread knife. 'They're getting closer. I expect that's why they're hiring more guards down at the City Museum. Better safe than sorry, eh?'

'You will be careful, won't you, Mum?' said Ben, a little anxiously. He didn't fancy the idea of his mum being alone at work in the museum with burglars about.

'Ha! It's those rotten robbers who need to be careful, now that your mum's on guard!' boomed Mr Pole proudly. He had given up on the bread knife and was taking a swing at his sausage with a meat cleaver. 'Isn't that right, my love?'

Mrs Pole ducked as the sausage pinged out from under the cleaver, shot past her at about eighty miles-per-hour, smashed through the kitchen window and landed in the back garden with a loud, solid *CLUNK!*

She smiled at Ben. 'I'll be fine, dear. At least there won't be any low-flying missiles to worry about,' she said, nodding at the banger that lay smouldering in the grass. 'You'll love the museum. You must come and visit. It's full of weird and wonderful things.'

'Is that where you got this, Dad?' grinned Ben, holding up his shrivelled sausage.

'Ah, erm . . . yes,' said Mr Pole sheepishly. 'How about some toast?'

Ben decided cornflakes would be the safest option. So he wolfed down a bowlful and headed out the door. It was the last day of his summer holidays, and he knew exactly where he wanted to be.

'Cheerio, love,' shouted Mrs Pole. 'Have fun, and say hello to Coo from us!'

Chapter Two

Ben knew the way off by heart by now. He slipped through the maze of alleys that ran between the high windowless buildings in the heart of the city. In a gloomy corner, down a dead-end, Ben swung back a loose board in a high wooden fence and squeezed through a small gap. It was dark on the other side.

Ben felt his way along a tunnel through a mass
of twisting roots and branches until at last they
thinned out, and he could see daylight shining at
the other end.

He stepped out into . . .

. . . Coo's magnificent woods.

Not many boys had a best friend like Coo. Ben was just lucky, he supposed. I mean, a *genius* who lives with a pet wombat in a *secret wood* in the middle of the city? In a *tree house*? He had to admit, it was pretty amazing! OK, so Coo's woods might be riddled with tricky traps and bonkers contraptions that were as dangerous as they were fun, but it was here that he felt most happy.

Ben couldn't wait to see Coo and Herbert again, but this time he was determined to reach Coo's tree house without stumbling into one of her traps. So, instead of running along the path like normal, Ben moved slowly and carefully, peering at the ground with every step.

And it worked, too. There, stretched across the path, he spotted a tripwire. Ben grinned and jumped over it.

27

Ben has stepped into...

The ZOOM of DOOM!

1. Ben steps on the switch
2. The SPRING shoots Ben up
3. He lands in the trolley
4. The trolley whooshes along the track
5. The trolley stops with a BUMP!
6. BEN falls out
7. BEN lands in the net

THUD!

SPROINGG!

CLICK!

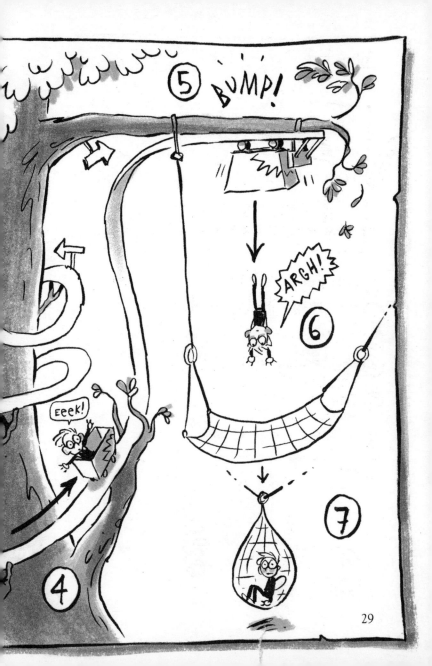

29

'Well, well, if it isn't Ben Pole,' said Coo, grinning at him from her perch on a branch above. 'You all right there? Need a hand?' she asked, her gold crown glinting in the sunlight and her long beard blowing in the breeze.

Ben groaned and looked up at her.

'Oh, OK, you got me again,' he said, giggling. 'The tripwire – it was a decoy, wasn't it?'

'Yup! You're learning, Pole,' said Coo, hopping down from the tree. 'You were pretty impressive, I think you hit a new top speed on that final bend.' She tugged a rope and the net fell open, dumping Ben in a heap on the ground. 'So, what do you think of the "ZOOM of DOOM"? Pretty good, eh?'

Ben groaned and held his head in both hands until everything stopped spinning.

'And you've turned up just in time,' Coo said, grabbing Ben and sitting him on a log. She fumbled about in her bag and pulled out a pair of odd-looking boots. 'Here, put these on.'

'Er, OK,' said Ben nervously. Coo's inventions had a nasty habit of being dangerous, so you can imagine how Ben felt, being a boy who thought mixing two flavours of ice cream was pretty risky.

'Hmm, not a bad fit,' Coo said, tightening the buckles of the strange boots.

'Right, follow me!'

'Hold on! What are these things? What do they do?' said Ben, picking up his bag and trotting awkwardly after his hairy friend as she shot off through the woods.

He caught up with her in a clearing a little further on.

It's no good giving me one of *those* looks, you fluffy lump. It's not *my* fault, is it?

'What's going on?' asked Ben. 'Who are you shouting at?'

'Oh, just that furry idiot up there. I tell you, sometimes I reckon he's got all the intelligence of a dim plum.'

Ben's gaze followed Coo's pointing finger into the highest branches of a tall silver-grey tree and there, clutching a slim branch and trembling with worry, was Herbert.

'Wombats are meant to BURROW IN THE GROUND, not CLIMB TREES, you DAFT PUDDING!' shouted Coo.

'How are you going to get him down?' asked Ben, shading his eyes against the glare of the white sky.

'I'm not.'

'Eh?'

'You are.'

'What? Me? No, I mean, I can't,' said Ben. 'All the way up there? You must be bonkers! Anyway, there's no way up, how would I even—'

'Oh, you'll manage,' grinned Coo crouching down and pressing a button on Ben's boots.

Ben shot straight up through the trees, leaving Coo far below.

'AAARGH! What's happening?' Ben screamed, as he came to a sudden shuddering halt. 'I don't like it, Coo! Get me down! What's going on?'

'Telescopic stilts, spring-loaded,' shouted Coo. 'Pretty sweet, eh?'

'NO!' wailed Ben. 'NOT sweet, actually! GET ME DOWN!'

'Grab Herb!' Coo shouted.

'What?'

'HERBERT! GRAB HIM!'

The skinny branch Herb was clinging to was barely

sturdy enough to bear the weight of a beefy sparrow, let alone a fat wombat. It bowed and creaked under the strain and looked likely to snap at any moment.

Ben's clumpy boots were tricky to walk in, but with a great effort he managed to swing his legs forward and totter over to Herbert.

As soon as Herb saw Ben, his rump began to wag with excitement.

Uh-oh, Ben thought, recognizing the look in Herb's eye.

'Now then, Herb, just wait there,' he said. 'I'm coming for you . . . No, no, NO! DON'T—'

Herb jumped.

He landed in Ben's arms, thumping against him like a furry wrecking ball.

Ben teetered on his long stilts, crashing back and forth through the treetops, desperately trying to keep his balance. He glanced at the ground and gulped. It was a LONG way down.

As he wobbled about, he could just see Coo far below, her hands cupped to her mouth, shouting up at him.

'Sick . . . poor . . . seals!'

'What?' Ben was so high up he could barely hear her.

'Lick . . . more . . . eels!'

'Lick more EELS?' shouted Ben. 'What do you mean, *lick more eels*? How on earth will THAT help?'

'CLICK . . . YOUR . . . *HEELS*!' yelled Coo as loud as she could.

'Oh, *HEELS*!' said Ben, finally making sense of it.

He clicked his boots together and, in a flash, the stilts retracted, shrinking Ben back down to ground level and dumping him and Herb on the soft leafy forest floor.

'Ha-ha! "Lick more eels"? You're crackers, Ben,' chuckled Coo as she patted Herb affectionately.

'CRACKERS? ME? You could have warned me! Ohhh my head. That was horrible.'

'You were brilliant, Pole. I knew you could do it.' Coo grinned, punching him on the shoulder. 'Those Stretch'n'Fetch Superboots worked a treat. I must admit, I had my doubts.'

'You mean they were untested? I could have been killed!'

'Well, they're tested now, aren't they? You don't half fuss, Ben,' said Coo. 'Herb loved it, didn't you, Herb? I think he wants another go.'

Ben flopped onto his back to catch his breath. Life was never dull with Coo around.

'Come on then,' Coo said, helping him up. 'You've earned yourself a ginger beer.'

CHAPTER THREE

Back at the tree house, Coo lit a fire and soon the hut was as warm as toast. Ben settled on a hammock with Herbert who curled up beside him for a nap.

'Oh, here, these are for you,' said Ben, digging a brown paper parcel from his bag.

'What is it?' said Coo, weighing the packet suspiciously in her hand.

'Sausages, apparently,' chuckled Ben. 'They're from Dad.'

'Er, thanks,' said Coo, the sausages clinking together as she tipped them into a bowl.

Herb raised his head from his folded paws, sniffed the air, shuddered ever so slightly and turned away.

'Oh well.' Coo grinned. 'Thanks anyway.'

Ben played about with Coo's ukulele while she poked at the fire with a stick and nibbled a handful of enormous roasted chestnuts.

'So, Mum started her new job today,' Ben said, 'at the museum.'

'Yeah? Great!' said Coo. 'Good timing too. Did y'hear? That Midnight Mob have struck again.'

'Yeah!' Ben was impressed. 'Hold on, how do you know about that?'

'I live in a tree house, Ben, not on the MOON,' said Coo with a wry smile. 'And I've got that there too,' she added, nodding over at an odd-fangled contraption with an enormous horn protruding from the top of it.

SOUND HORN →

Winding handle ↘

→ 'ON'

CONKER tone RADIOGRAM

'Is that a . . . a radio?' said Ben taking a closer look and twiddling a big wooden knob.

'Of course it's a radio,' said Coo. 'This IS the twenty-first century, you know.'

'I'm going to miss this,' sighed Ben, sitting back on the hammock and scratching Herbert behind the ears. 'School starts tomorrow. Mum wants me to join an after-school club now that she's working too. I won't be able to come over so much.'

'Well, since it's the last day of your holidays, how about some ice skating?' said Coo with that kind of sidelong smile that made Ben suspect that she needed another contraption testing.

'Er, of course I'd love to, Coo, yeah nothing better, but we can't, can we?' said Ben with obvious relief. 'The pond isn't frozen.'

'Yeah, maybe not,' said Coo, crossing to a work-bench. She picked up a strange backpack with a hose thingummy-jig hanging off the side, heaved it onto her shoulders, fastened a buckle on the front and winked at Ben.

But it will be!

CHAPTER FOUR

The following morning Ben found himself back at school. It was a brand-new term and the feeling had just about returned to his toes after the Snow'n'Blow incident the day before.

During the holidays the school had been scrubbed clean. The whole place smelled of floor wax and the corridors bustled with packs of new kids who milled about in their big shiny shoes and oversized blazers.

The bell rang for assembly, and Ben shuffled into the main hall with everyone else and sat near the back. The kids all fidgeted and chatted noisily. Ben was just admiring the excellent aim of a boy who had managed to clonk a kid at the front with a perfectly lobbed cheese roll when . . .

It was Mr Gigglethwick, the headmaster. The gap in his front teeth might have meant that he couldn't play the bassoon with any confidence, but he could whistle loud enough to shatter glass at a hundred metres.

'Right then, you lot, simmer down, simmer down,' he said in a loud voice. 'That's better. Well, good morning, children. Welcome to a new school year.'

While the headmaster droned on, Ben's concentration wandered. He enjoyed a few moments imagining Coo building him a cheese-roll catapult. He was just considering which type of cheese would be most aerodynamic when his attention snapped back to what the headmaster was saying. He had mentioned something about a *'disaster'*.

'The police still aren't certain how it happened,' said Mr Gigglethwick. 'I mean, it's not clear what Mr Travis was even doing in the pudding factory last night, let alone how he fell into the vat of boiling jelly.

'If only he'd landed in the cream and custard tub or on one of those slabs of soft sponge cake he might not have been hurt so badly. It's all a trifle baffling.

'Anyway, until Mr Travis has all his bandages removed, I'm afraid he won't be here to run the History Club. I'm sure we all hope he gets well soon.

'Now, before we finish, I would like to introduce you to some special guests. Please welcome Professor Pickering and his pupils from the Lilly Lavender Private Academy for Exceptional Girls.'

Ben craned his neck for a better view as Mr Gigglethwick beckoned a tall man and four girls to join him on the stage.

'Good morning, Professor Pickering,' the children chanted all together.

Professor Pickering smiled and bowed. His head was bald on top and fringed with curly hair, he wore a tweed jacket with elbow patches and he even had a wonky eye. The girls stood in a row beside him. Their school uniform was pink and yellow, and they peered out shyly from beneath straw hats tied with ribbons.

'The professor and the girls will be spending some time here at our school as part of a project they are working on; comparing all the schools around the city,' explained Mr Gigglethwick. 'So, make them feel welcome. And be good,' he added sternly, glaring at the boy who had thrown the cheese roll.

'Thaaaank you, headmaster,' said Pickering smoothly, smiling at the assembled children.

'We look forward to a happy time here with you all at your school. May I say how dreadfully sorry I am to hear about your poor Mr Travis,' the professor added, bowing his head. 'It so happens that I run a History Club too, at the Lilly Lavender Academy.' He turned to Mr Gigglethwick. 'If you don't mind, I'd be happy to run your History Club while Mr Travis is still in his . . . *ahem* . . . sticky situation.'

'Well that will be wonderful, professor, won't it, children?' Mr Gigglethwick beamed. 'Thank you.'

The professor bowed and the girls curtsied awkwardly before returning to their seats.

'Marvellous!' said Mr Gigglethwick. 'Right then, children, off you go! Hurry up! Time for your lessons.'

CHAPTER FIVE

Ben emerged from his final lesson of the day feeling dazed and clutching a list of homework as long as his arm.

He wanted to go back to the woods and drink cold ginger beer in front of a hot fire with Coo and Herb, but he had promised his mum that he'd join an after-school club so he wandered over to the noticeboards to see what was on offer.

His heart sank. Nothing seemed any fun at all.

He was just about to give up, shut his eyes and pick one at random when he remembered what Professor Pickering had said in assembly. He decided that History Club had to be better than 'Basket-weaving-with-drinking-straws Club'. After all, his mum had been raving about how amazing the museum was, and that was packed with historical things. So with his mind made up, Ben headed to Mr Travis's classroom.

Mᶜ TRAVIS

When he got there, he could hear voices and see shadows moving about through the pane of frosted glass in the door.

He knocked gingerly.

The voices stopped talking.

The door opened and a small girl with curly blonde hair and a big nose looked up at Ben from under her straw hat.

'Hello?' she squeaked.

'Er, is this the History Club?' asked Ben, glancing past her. 'I want to sign up. Professor Pickering said—'

'We're full up,' said the girl curtly and she slammed the door shut.

Ben stood there for a moment and then knocked once more.

There was a murmur of whispered conversation beyond the door and then it opened again.

Professor Pickering looked at Ben with his good
eye.

'I'm frightfully sorry about that. My girls are a
little . . . shy. So, who are you, dear boy?' he said
with a kind smile.

'Er, I'm Ben Pole,' said Ben peering past the professor. All four of the academy girls were sitting at a table taking their pink notebooks from their yellow satchels and arranging them neatly beside their glittery felt-tip pens. 'I was, um, hoping to join your history club.'

'Oh. Ah, yes.' Professor Pickering sucked air in through his teeth. 'Well, it's only a small club and as you can see—'

'It's just that my mum works at the museum,' said Ben. 'As a security guard.'

'Does she really?' interrupted the professor. 'How marvellous! We were just now planning a field trip to the museum, weren't we, girls?'

'Yes, Professor Pickering,' said the girls eagerly.

Professor Pickering put a friendly arm around Ben's shoulder and drew him into the classroom.

'You know, perhaps your mum might help us arrange our little field trip?'

'Ooh,' squeaked a girl with ginger braids that bounced as she bobbed up and down with excitement,

Can we have a V.I.P. tour? Behind the scenes and everything?

And what about the gift shop? Is there a gift shop?

With **Unicorn** Pencil toppers?

'Now then, girls, calm down,' said Pickering, turning to Ben. 'Let the boy speak.'

'Yes, of course.' Ben smiled. 'I'll ask Mum. She'll be happy to help.'

'Well, that's settled then,' said Pickering, patting Ben on the shoulder. 'I'm sure we can make room in our little club for one more. Come and meet the girls.'

The girls clapped their hands and made space for Ben at the table.

'Your timing is perfect,' said Pickering. 'We were just about to open a packet of chocolate biscuits and chat about the invention of explosives by the Chinese back in the tenth century.'

Now then, who has the dynamite?

The History Club was fun. Not as fun as mucking about in the woods, but it wasn't a bad way to spend the afternoons.

Yes, it might have had something to do with Professor Pickering's habit of handing out chocolate biscuits willy-nilly, but he was full of exciting stories too, about pirates, thieves and scallywags throughout history.

Coo would enjoy these, thought Ben, chomping into a Double-Chocolate Crumblie, especially the one about Fizz-Bang Fitzwilliam the Inventor Thief, whose clockwork gang terrorized Victorian London.

What's more, there was never a dull moment with the professor and his wonky eye. Up close Ben could see that it was a fake. It wasn't even glass. It was a ping-pong ball with a black dot drawn on it. Most of the time you wouldn't notice, but now and then it would dry out and get stuck at a funny angle so he would be looking at Ben with one eye and staring at the ceiling with the other.

Then Professor Pickering would lick the tip of his pinky, poke it in his eye and swivel it back into position with a wet *sqrweek* sound. It was hilarious! Revolting, but hilarious!

Sqrweeeeeeeeeek!

The girls were friendly too. They fussed around Ben, offering to paint his nails glitter pink and spritz him with puffs of Princess Pony perfume. It was a bit much, but Ben didn't mind. Even Petal, the shy girl in the group, warmed to him, offering him a sniff of her strawberry-scented pencil-topper.

As promised, Ben's mum arranged a tour of the City Museum and on Wednesday afternoon Ben gave his club mates the good news.

'It's all set for tomorrow,' he said. 'The trip!'

The professor was delighted. The girls squealed with excitement.

'Excellent!' said Professor Pickering. 'I'll arrange for a bus to pick us up. Don't be late! It's going to be marvellous!'

CHAPTER SIX

On a bright Thursday afternoon, the school minibus shuddered to a halt in front of the museum.

'Yoo-hoo! Ben!' Mrs Pole waved from the entrance at the top of the steps.

'Hi, Mum,' said Ben, trotting up to meet her. 'This is Professor Pickering.'

'Mrs Pole, my dear lady,' said Professor Pickering, stepping forward and shaking Mrs Pole's hand. 'Thank you so very much for arranging this field trip for our little club. We are awfully grateful, aren't we?' he added, shoving the girls forward.

'Yes, professor, thank you, madam,' they said all at once, curtsying awkwardly and fluttering their eyelashes.

'Oh, er, that's quite all right. I'm happy to help,' said Mrs Pole, giving Ben a sideways smile and raising an eyebrow.

Mrs Pole led them on a tour of the museum, pointing out her favourite exhibits. They walked through galleries filled with huge skeletons and stuffed creatures from all over the world, along corridors lined with glass cabinets gleaming with polished suits of armour and swords, and into crypts where dazzling butterflies and green-gold beetles the size of dinner plates glittered and flashed under the spotlights.

Horrible shrunken heads dangled from hooks and shrivelled hands lay in silk-lined boxes. Paintings and tapestries covered the walls and mannequins wearing silver crowns and velvet gowns stood in every corner.

They wandered the length and breadth of the museum, and just as Ben began to feel that it must be time for a rest, a glass of lemonade and a bun, Mrs Pole stopped beside a pair of enormous doors and turned to the little group.

'I've saved the best until last,' she said, smiling with anticipation. 'This weekend our latest and greatest exhibition opens to the public here in the Treasure Chamber. As a special treat, you get to have a sneaky peek before anyone else. It's still being set up, I'm afraid, but I think you'll like it. Here it is,' she said, opening the doors.

The enormous chamber was being prepared for the exhibition. Fake jungle creepers clung to the pillars, and in the centre of it all were piles of packing cases stuffed with riches.

'I say!' gasped Pickering. 'How wonderful!'

'The Mummy's Gold belongs to the tribe of the Blue-foots, so-called on account of their blue feet,' explained Mrs Pole as the little group looked around.

The Blue-foots have lived deep in the jungles of South America for hundreds of years. Their land was once rich in gold and jewels and they made the most beautiful and dazzling treasure. Other tribes tried to steal it. But Mighty Ozozo, the wise and powerful medicine man of the Blue-foots, used his magic to save the treasure every time. When he died, to honour him, he was mummified and buried in a tomb with all the treasure of the Blue-foots. That treasure is the Mummy's Gold you see here.

How did it end up here?

89

Well, with Mighty Ozozo gone, it was stolen from the Blue-foots by a gang of thieves and was believed to be lost for ever, until just recently. Much to the delight of the current chief of the Blue-foots, Chief Umpopo, some explorers found it stashed in an abandoned jungle temple. Chief Umpopo is coming to take the treasure home to his tribe. He kindly agreed to let us exhibit it first. It's very exciting! We will present him with the gold at the opening of the exhibition.

'What an extraordinary story,' said Professor Pickering as he circled the room with Ben and the girls, gazing at the wonderful treasures they could see poking out from the crates.

Gold cups and plates glinted in the light. Jewelled bracelets, necklaces and rings flashed with colour. Golden statues peeped out from their wrappings. And in the centre of it all, in a padded box, they even glimpsed a golden skull.

The gleaming gold bathed their faces in shimmering yellow light.

'So all that gold is REAL?' asked Ben, his eyes as wide as saucers.

'Oh yes, love,' said his mum. 'Pure gold.'

'Twenty-four carat,' said Lovely Susan.

'Yes, and look at those perfect sapphires, emeralds and rubies,' added Daisy, her big nose inches from the crates. 'They're flawless.'

'Gosh!' said Mrs Pole, impressed. 'You are clever girls, aren't you? Just wait until you see the Mummy's Crown! It is the star of the show! It will take your breath away, but it's still packed up just now. You'll have to come back to see it in the exhibition. You're quite right though, Daisy. The gems are perfect. The treasure must be worth—'

'Three hundred and sixty-nine million, one hundred and eighty-two thousand, four hundred and sixty-nine pounds and twenty-seven pence,' said Professor Pickering. 'Give or take,' he added, sidling up to Mrs Pole.

'A treasure so valuable must be awfully well protected,' he said casually, slipping a camera from his pocket and taking a few snaps.

'Oh crikey, absolutely!' said Mrs Pole.

'Oh, I hope so,' said Daisy, fluttering her eye-lashes. 'It's *so* pretty.'

'Don't worry, love. It's safe and sound. Let's see, firstly, all the doors and windows are locked up tight at night. Then there are all the cameras to spot any burglars, and there are alarms too. The doors to the Treasure Chamber are made of three-inch-thick steel and have auto-lock timers. And, of course,' said Mrs Pole, puffing out her chest, 'there's me. I'm more than a match for any pesky burglar.'

'No one's going to get past you, Mum,' said Ben proudly.

'Thanks, love,' said Mrs Pole. 'I'm not worried. I mean, who'd want to steal the treasure anyway? Apparently it's cursed.'

'So they say. Now THAT would make a good project for your club,' said Mrs Pole. 'You can look it up in one of your books. Ben is fascinated by curses, ghosts and all that stuff.' She smiled at Professor Pickering, rolling her eyes. 'Boys will be boys.'

'That's a smashing idea,' said Professor Pickering. 'Something to think about for next term, eh girls? Right! Come along then,' he said briskly, clapping his hands together. 'Time to go, I think. Ben will want to be off home for his tea and I'm sure Mrs Pole has plenty to be getting on with. So, girls, what do you say to the dear lady?'

'Thank you, Mrs Pole,' they said all together, bobbing with wobbly curtsies.

'You're welcome.' Mrs Pole beamed. 'And please come again, won't you?'

'Oh, we will, Mrs Pole,' oozed Professor Pickering as they waved goodbye. 'We will. Cheerio, Ben, my boy, see you tomorrow.'

EEPBEEPBEEEPBEE

PEEPBEEPEE

CHAPTER SEVEN

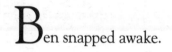

Ben snapped awake.

BEEPE EEPBEEPBE

'NOW what?' he groaned, dragging himself out of bed. He pulled on his dressing gown and plodded downstairs.

EPBEEPBEEPBEEP BEE

Ben's nose twitched with the now familiar smell of burnt breakfast wafting from the kitchen.

'DAD? IS THAT YOU?' he shouted, pressing his fingers into his ears to block out the noise.

BEEP-WHACK!-BE PBEEP

KEEP YOUR VOICE DOWN, LAD!

Mr Pole was standing on a stool and whacking the shrieking smoke alarm with a broom.

YOUR MUM'S SLEEPING! SHE'S WORKING TONIGHT! IT'S HER FIRST NIGHTSHIFT AT THE MUSEUM!

'JUST PRESS THE RED BUTTON,' yelled Ben, wafting the back door open and closed to clear the smoke, 'TO TURN IT OFF!'

'WHAT D'YOU SAY?' boomed Mr Pole, giving up on the broom and wrenching the smoke alarm down from the ceiling. It warbled weakly in his hands and sputtered into silence.

'Never mind,' said Ben.

'Mum made me put in fresh batteries,' said Mr Pole, holding up the alarm.

Apparently I'm a fire hazard.

'On breakfast duty again then?' said Ben, peering cautiously at the blackened pan on the stove. The *green* smoke didn't fill him with confidence.

'Yup!' grinned his dad proudly. 'It's PORRIDGE this morning!'

So, one slice or two?

Mr Pole's porridge was the kind of porridge that would be perfect if you needed something to dam up a river, or stick heavy tiles to a roof on a windy day, but it wasn't the sort of thing a boy ought to be eating for breakfast. It was so gluey that Ben spent the first half of the school day with his jaws firmly stuck together. He couldn't utter a sound. In his chemistry lesson, he even got a gold star from Mrs Haversack for *sitting quietly* because he was the only boy to not make loud farty noises during her slideshow about gases.

Ben couldn't even manage lunch, and spent the afternoon picking the last globs of porridge from between his back teeth with the tip of a pencil.

But Ben was happy.

The weekend was just around the corner and that morning his dad had cheerfully agreed to let him skip History Club and sleep over at Coo's place, so he'd soon be back in the woods tucking into some delicious grub beside a roaring fire. Ben's stomach gurgled joyfully at the thought of it.

After his last lesson of the day, Ben trotted over to Mr Travis's classroom to see Professor Pickering and excuse himself from History Club.

When he got there the room was empty, so Ben let himself in and scrawled a quick note to leave on the professor's desk.

His empty stomach burbled loudly, and suddenly all Ben could think of was Professor Pickering's chocolate biscuits.

The professor was so generous, thought Ben, he wouldn't mind if Ben took just *one*, would he? Ben's eyes were drawn to the storeroom door in the back wall. He probably kept them in there, he thought, his stomach gurgling again.

Before he knew it, he had slipped through the door and was searching the little room. He had just grabbed a packet of Double-Chocolate Crumblies from a top shelf when he heard the classroom door creak open and several feet shuffle in.

Mr TRAVIS

Ben froze. He suddenly felt terribly guilty. What would the professor think if he caught Ben stealing? He put the biscuits back and crouched behind the door to hide until the coast was clear.

He expected to hear the chatter and squeals of the academy girls, but it was eerily quiet. Ben strained his ears to listen. A cold shiver ran down his spine when the silence was broken by the low, gruff whispers of men.

109

Ben froze in horror as something white, wet and round rolled to a standstill just inside the storeroom door and *stared up at him*.

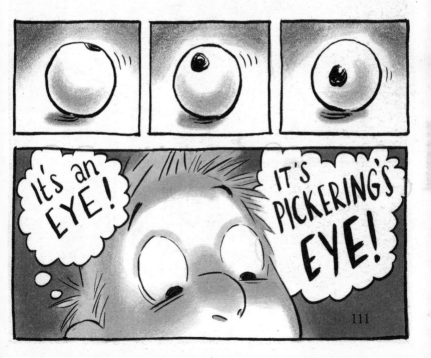

111

Ben sat glued to the spot not daring to move a muscle until he heard the men shuffle back out of the classroom. Then he waited in the shadows some more until he was sure he was alone.

Ben felt dizzy. What was Pickering up to? Who were those men? He couldn't think. It had all happened so fast.

One thing was certain.

He needed help.

He needed a genius.

He needed King Coo.

COOOOOOOOOOooo!

CHAPTER EIGHT

Ben stood at the edge of the wood
and shouted into the trees.
This was an emergency!

'Hello, Pole! What's up?'

'You made me jump!' Ben yelped. 'HOW do you get around SO fast?'

'I can hear you coming a mile off.' Coo grinned. 'You're about as stealthy as a moose on stilts. Wearing clogs. And a hat with bells on. Are you OK? You look frazzled,' she added. 'Let's get you a drink, and you can tell me what's going on.'

All the way to the tree house, Ben gabbled about
everything that had happened. He barely stopped
to take a breath as it all spilled out. Coo grabbed
his elbow, sat him by the fire and put a mug
of ginger beer in his hand, and all the while Ben
chattered on. He told Coo everything, from the
first time he saw Pickering at assembly, right up to
the horrible moment of the eye staring up at him in
the storeroom.

'So, let me get this straight,' she said when Ben had finished talking and was sitting breathless on the edge of his seat. 'You think this Pickering is the boss of the Midnight Mob?'

'I'm not sure,' said Ben. 'It was definitely Pickering, and the men definitely sounded dodgy. They're planning something, for tonight! And, blimey, what about the girls? They might be in danger! We have to do something!'

'Have you got any proof?' said Coo, leaning forward, twiddling her beard thoughtfully.

'No, nothing,' sighed Ben. 'But I saw the gold coin! I'm sure I did. It must have been stolen from the Viking Museum that was in the news. It was big and old-looking.'

'Hmmmm.' Coo frowned, deep in thought. 'That reminds me of something . . . Hold on!' she said.

She crossed to Herbert's beanbag, where he lay snoozing, and heaved him to one side.

119

She rummaged through a small pile of bottle caps, foil sweet wrappers and other bits and bobs.

'I KNEW it!' she said triumphantly, standing up and flicking something across the room to Ben.

PING

It flashed in the light and landed with a heavy thump on Ben's lap – it was a FAT GOLD COIN.

'What . . . wait . . . how . . . ?' Ben spluttered. The coin gleamed as he turned it over in his hands.

This is the SAME as the one I saw!

'It's Herbert,' said Coo. 'He *loves* shiny things. He finds all sorts when he's out digging. He came back this morning looking especially pleased with himself.'

Herbert trotted over and bumped against Coo's legs affectionately.

'I only got a glimpse of it, but I should have guessed you'd found something good, eh fella?' she said, giving his smiling chops a loving scratch.

Coo grinned and clapped her hands together. 'This is going to be so much fun!' she said, grabbing a spear and hoisting her bag on to her shoulder.

Coo took the coin from Ben and held it under Herbert's velvety nose.

'Now, I know that most of the time Herb looks like a hairy pillow with a leg at each corner, but he's actually a really good tracker. If he can show us where he got this, it might give us some answers.'

Herb snuffled the coin for a moment. Then he tipped his head to the open door, sniffed the breeze, and shot off like a cuddly rocket.

Woo-Hoo! Come on, Pole!

Running as fast as they could,
they followed Herbert along the
broad branches and high walk-
ways that wound through the
treetops.

They whooshed
down slides to the mossy forest
floor and ran on after Herbert
as he crashed through tall ferns
and thick undergrowth. Every now
and then he would pause to sniff the
air, before dashing off in a fresh
direction. Ben had never been this far from

the tree house before. It was dark and damp. The wet leaves squelched beneath his feet and the tall thin trees cut out the faint autumn light as they neared the edge of the woods.

Suddenly, the ground dipped steeply and Ben and Coo found themselves following Herb into a narrow ravine. The rocky walls were slimy, with dark green moss and twisted tree roots.

They paused for breath when they reached the far end. Ben looked up and froze.

CHAPTER NINE

They were standing in front of a gloomy, dripping cave, the rocky edges black and sharp like enormous rotten teeth.

'You're not scared of the dark are you, Pole?' said Coo, rummaging around in her bag.

'No!' said Ben, a little too quickly. 'Well, only *dark* dark,' he admitted. 'I'm fine with *light* dark.'

'Ha! You're brilliant, Ben! Bonkers!' said Coo. 'Well, don't worry. We can use one of these,' she added, pulling out a glowing jar of fireflies and tying it to the tip of her spear.

The faint light of Coo's firefly lantern skipped and flittered across the glistening walls and ceiling of the cave as Herbert led them inside and down a narrow passage.

'It looks like we're going deep. Grab Herbert for a minute, will you, and come with me,' said Coo as she stepped through a side-passage into a large cavern.

Here we are. I just need to grab something from the Mush Room.

Coo beamed. 'I grow them. They're from all over the world. And there's a few I whipped up myself,' she added, proudly patting the trunk of the most gigantic blue mushroom Ben had ever seen.

'They're really useful,' said Coo, pointing out a few favourites. 'Those make good medicine, those ones inflate and float in the air, and those ones explode.'

'It's fantastic!' said Ben.

'A-ha! *These* are the ones I've been looking for.'
Coo stepped up to a fungus that looked like a giant
marshmallow stuck to the cave wall, tore off two
large pieces and threw one to Ben.

It felt cool and spongy in his hands.

'Oh, great! I'm starving,' he said, having felt
hungry ever since his dad had taken over the
cooking.

'Oh crikey, don't EAT it!' said Coo. 'It'll bring
you out in spots and you'll not know which way is
up for days! No, squeeze it hard, and shake it.'

Ben squashed it. He felt it pop and crackle inside
and grow warm. Then he shook it
hard with both hands and
to his delight it burst
into bright green
light.

'Ha-ha! That's . . . that's . . . AMAZING!'
Ben grinned, whirling the mushroom around his
head and splashing the floor with glowing juice.

'I call them Glowshrooms,' said Coo, squashing
and shaking her own one to life. 'Not bad, eh?'

'Now come on,' she said, sticking the Glowshroom
on to the tip of her spear. 'There's no time to muck
about.'

Leaving the Mush Room behind them, Ben
and Coo followed Herbert as he padded off into
the dark. The path snaked and dipped through
caves big and small, squeezing through cracks
tight enough to make their ribs squeak, and
through caverns large enough to
comfortably hold a football
pitch, a multiplex cinema
and probably a bowling
alley too, if you stood
it up on one end.

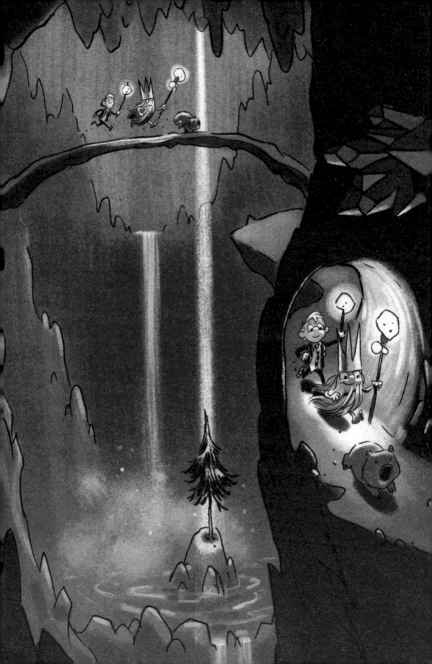

Eventually, they ducked into a passageway that seemed to shrink with every step until the ceiling was so low that Coo and Ben were forced to crawl behind Herbert on their hands and knees.

'He's slowing down,' said Coo. 'We're close.'

A moment later they emerged from the other end onto a narrow ledge.

Herbert stopped, turned to Coo and wagged his rump.

'This is it!' said Coo. 'This is where Herb found the coin.'

Beneath them was a large cave. Faint daylight seeped in from a tunnel on the far side.

'Well, it looks like *someone's* been up to mischief!' said Coo.

Heaped against one wall there was a big black bag, stuffed to bursting with gold coins that spilled across the floor, and stuck to the walls were photos, maps and plans of all the museums that had been burgled.

'Blimey! It's the Midnight Mob!' gasped Ben.

Suddenly, a rock clattered along the tunnel opposite.

'Someone's coming!' whispered Coo.

They ducked down low and peeked over the ledge.

CHAPTER TEN

Five shadowy figures came into view – four short ones and a tall one.

'It's the girls!' hissed Ben into Coo's ear. 'Pickering's caught the girls!'

Daisy, Petal, Primrose and Lovely Susan tripped and skidded down into the cave. Behind them came Pickering. His fake eye had slipped all the way round and it shone horribly white in the dim light.

'We've got to help them!' said Ben, getting to his feet.

'Hold on!' whispered Coo, clamping a hand around Ben's mouth and pulling him back down. She sat as still as a hawk and watched from the ledge through narrowed eyes.

'Light the lamps,' ordered Pickering in the gloom, 'I can't see a thing.'

His voice was harsh now. Gone was the smooth chuckling professor who had seemed so friendly.

Yellow lamplight lit up the cave, casting flickering shadows across the rocky walls.

Ben, Coo and Herb sank lower.

The academy girls gathered around Pickering.

Then Daisy spoke. 'Is it safe, professor?'

Ben shot a questioning glance at Coo.

Pickering checked the tunnel and cocked an ear to listen.

Silence.

'Yes, all clear,' he said.

Then he smacked himself on the back of his head, popping the ping-pong ball out into his hand.

WHACK!
POP!

'Don't worry,' he said, holding it up. 'I'll keep an *eye* out for trouble.'

The girls all burst into horrible laughter.

PAH-HA-HA-HA-HA-HA!

'Ha! It's about flippin' time!' said Petal. 'These knickers don't half pinch!'

'And these perishing *shoes*! Torture!' Lovely Susan groaned. 'I've got toes like mashed plums.'

Ben gawped in disbelief as they tossed their hats away and threw off their blazers and skirts. They kicked off their shiny little shoes and tugged their blouses over their heads.

'Yeah, and my throat's red raw from speaking like this all the time!' squeaked Daisy, cough-ing a few times until her voice dropped to a low grumble.

KAF! KAF!
KAF! KAF!
KAF!

'Aaaah, what a relief! This itches like mad!' Primrose sighed, snatching her hair from her head.

The girls were gone. Their disguises littered the cave floor.

Ben stared down from the ledge.

'Crikey! They're not girls at all!' he whispered to Coo, unable to tear his eyes away.

CHAPTER ELEVEN

'Well done, *girls*! Phase one is complete! It works every time!' said Pickering triumphantly, putting on an eye patch. He twirled on the spot, flapping his hands and fluttering his eyelids.

'No one ever suspects *the Professor and his Academy Girls!*'

The men rocked with laughter. 'Ha-ha! Nice one, boss!'

'And we mustn't forget the *oh-so-helpful* Poles,' said Pickering, clasping his hands to his heart. 'Those dopes made it easier than ever for us to get a sneaky peek at the treasure and plan tonight's little adventure. Speaking of which,' he said, pulling a fresh bottle of rum from a crate, 'we strike at midnight!'

He pointed at each of them in turn. 'It's the same as last time, lads. DODGE, you get us in through the skylight; SHIFTY, you fritz the alarms; JELLY, you get us through the time-lock doors to the Treasure Chamber; and CRUSHER, you're on lookout. Got it?'

'Got it, boss.'

'Good lads,' said Pickering, pulling the cork from the bottle with a squeaky *POP* and sloshing rum into cups. 'A toast,' he said, raising his cup. 'THE MIDNIGHT MOB!'

'Well, well, well,' Pickering said. 'Followed us, did you, Pole? SPYING on us, were you?'

'Er. No,' said Ben feebly. 'Um, I was just passing . . .'

Pickering looked suspiciously up at the ledge from where Ben had tumbled. 'Dodge, Crusher! Quick! Go and check! He might not be alone.'

They scampered up to the ledge and out of sight.

'Shifty, tie him up.'

'Is it time for another *accident* at the pudding factory?' said Shifty gleefully, tying Ben's hands with elaborate knots. 'He must've heard everything.'

'I didn't!' said Ben. 'Honest! You don't even *look* like robbers! Oh, er, I mean, um, I don't know anything! I really ought to be getting home . . . Let me go, please! I won't tell! You don't need to drag me along, I'll just get in your way!'

'Ha! Thank you, Pole, what an excellent idea,' grinned Pickering. 'You're coming with us to rob the museum!'

'What? No!' Ben wriggled desperately.

'Oh yes you are, Benny-boy,' said Pickering. 'You're going to be our little hostage, so if we bump into your mum, she won't be any trouble, will she? Not if she doesn't want anything bad to happen to *you*, that is!'

158

'There's no one there, boss!' said Dodge and Crusher, skidding back down from the ledge.

'There was some footprints, but they disappeared over the edge of a pit. If there was anyone there, they'll be a splotch at the bottom by now.'

Pickering smiled cruelly at Ben. 'Well, it looks like you're on your own, chum.'

'Please!' Ben pleaded. 'I don't want to go! What about the CURSE? I don't want to be shrivelled!'

Jelly nudged Crusher. 'The squirt's gone doolally. Crazy in the coconut.'

'No! Remember what my mum said?' insisted Ben.

Pickering scoffed. 'Only a pudding-brain would believe that piffle.'

'Heh-heh! Yeah!' nodded Dodge and Jelly, glancing sideways at each other. 'Pudding-brains, yeah.'

'So we're going, right?' said Pickering, staring at each of them in turn before swivelling his eye towards Ben. 'And *you* are coming too, got it?'

Ben nodded feebly.

'Well then,' he said, 'break it up and get some rest, you lot!

CHAPTER TWELVE

M idnight.

The moon peeped out from behind silver clouds and cast a pale white light over the City Museum.

Six dark figures scurried silently across the roof.

They stopped beside a skylight and peered through it to the entrance hall far below.

Ben stared into the inky blackness. He turned to Pickering. 'It's not too late,' he whispered desperately. 'If we leave now the curse won't get us!'

'Quiet!' hissed Pickering fiercely, his single eye glinting in the moonlight.

Dodge cut a neat hole in the glass, just big enough for him to slip a hand through and flip the window catch.

One by one, the gang clipped
themselves to a rope,
slipped over the edge and
slid down through the open
skylight into the huge dark
hall beneath them.
'Now you, Pole,' snarled
Pickering, and he shoved
Ben backwards through
the window.
Ben whizzed down the
rope. At the bottom, rough
hands caught him, lashed a
rope around his waist and
held him close like a dog on
a short leash. Pickering
was the last one down.

'OK, lads,' he whispered, clicking on his head-torch. 'Follow me, and don't make a sound.'

They set off through the dark.

CLICK...click...clicketty....clack..cl

'Quiet, I said!' hissed Pickering. 'Not a peep!'

Clicketty...clacketty...CLICK...CLA

'I thought I told you to shut it!' he hissed again.

'Muh-me t-t-too,' trembled Jelly. 'I'm fuh-fuh-fuh-freezing.'

'Oh n-n-n-no! It's the f-fever!' said Ben, shivering in the dark.

Pickering's torch lit up Ben's frightened face.

The gang looked nervously at Pickering.

'It's an old b-b-building, Pole,' he said. 'A damp old building and n-nothing more. Now c-come on, let's move. It's this way.' He tugged on Ben's rope and dragged him out of the hall.

They turned the corner and stepped into a long and deserted corridor. Pickering paused. Tiny red lights blinked in every dark corner.

'Cameras,' he whispered. 'Shifty, you're up.'

'Yes, b-boss.' Shifty nodded. He dropped to the ground and slithered on his belly like a fat adder to tinker with a small black junction box bolted to the wall.

There was a flash and a crackle and all the cameras blinked off.

Shifty gave Pickering the all clear. 'The alarms are fritzed too, boss.'

'Excellent!' Pickering grinned. 'Let's go!'

Their torchlight flickered and bobbed in the dark as they snuck through a hall full of statues,

stuffed animals and ornate suits of armour
that gleamed in the pale moonlight
streaming in from the high
windows. Pickering led the
way, dragging Ben after
him. Dodge, Shifty,
Crusher and Jelly
followed close behind.

173

'Hey, Dodge,' whispered Crusher, nudging Dodgy Dave in the ribs. 'What's up with the squirt?'

Dodge shone his light at Ben who was muttering to himself and darting nervous glances around the room.

'He's off his chump!' said Dodge. 'He looks potty to me.'

'C-can you see them?' Ben blurted out. 'They're everywhere!'

'What now?' said Pickering, spinning round. 'I told you to keep quiet!'

'W-warnings!' Ben pointed a trembling finger. 'Look! All around us! Horrible!'

'You must be seeing things!' sneered Pickering, shining his torch around. 'There's nothing there.'

'Seeing things?' said Crusher. His voice wobbled. 'What, like in the CURSE?'

'Oh no! It's the SECOND sign!' Jelly gazed into the dark. 'I SEE 'EM TOO! Turn off your lights!'

One by one the gang switched off their torches.

They blinked and rubbed their eyes. Jelly's voice echoed in the gloom.

See?

TERROR AWAITS YOU!

Words had appeared, and pictures too, scrawled across the floor and up the walls. They glimmered green, glowing eerily in the dark.

LEAVE OR BE SHRIVELLED

Ben pulled at the rope around his waist. 'Let me go, Pickering! I don't want to get SHRIVELLED!'

'QUIET, POLE!' hissed Pickering, yanking Ben close. 'A mummy's curse will be the least of your problems if you don't stop wriggling and do what I say!'

'And that goes for the rest of you, too!' he snarled under his breath. 'We're going to steal that treasure. No trick of the light's going to stop us! Got it?'

'Yes, boss,' mumbled the gang, still staring wide-eyed at the glowing warnings.

Pickering strode forward, pulling Ben with him. The gang scampered after them, anxious to get the gold and get away as fast as they could.

They crept on, along corridors and up wide marble stairs. At last, they came to the huge metal doors of the Treasure Chamber. They were locked tight.

'This is it, lads!' said Pickering in an excited whisper.

Jelly, do your stuff. Get us in!

'Yes, boss,' said Jelly, slipping his cutting torch from his shoulder. He fired it up, adjusted its flame to a hot blue point and started work.

Ben had to shield his eyes from the bright sparks that spat and fizzed from the door as Jelly began to cut. When he was done, a large wobbly circle glowed orange on the door. Jelly gave it a sharp kick and it fell inwards, landing with a CLANG on the other side.

Pickering bent down and stepped through the hole in the doors, dragging Ben behind him. The others followed, taking care not to burn themselves on the hot, glowing edges.

'Well, gentlemen,' said Pickering, throwing his arms wide, 'here it is.'

CHAPTER THIRTEEN

They gasped. The crates and packing cases were gone. The treasure was on glorious display.

It was utterly magnificent! It was mind-bogglingly, *eye-gogglingly* amazing! (If there was such a word as '*eye-gogglingly*', that is.)

If all the treasures of the world were each marked out of ten, then the Mummy's Gold would score a solid one hundred and seven. Out of ten. That's how incredible it was. It might possibly even score one hundred and eight, if the judge was particularly fond of enormous diamonds.

Golden trinkets, goblets and daggers, all glittering with jewels, spilled from chests. Gold statues stood guard, draped in tribal robes and clutching ornate clubs studded with precious stones. Dazzling treasures were on display in every direction and in the centre of it all, perched on a golden skull, was the Mummy's Crown.

It gleamed in the torchlight.

Pickering caught his breath.

'Look! There in the centre!' he said, pointing at the crown. 'That diamond! It's the size of a goose egg!'

'A big goose,' added Dodge in an awed whisper. 'A big, fat goose.'

The gang gazed greedily at the treasure, their fears forgotten.

Pickering snapped into action.

Quick! The bags!
Fill them up, lads!
Fill them to the brim!

They were over the ropes
in a flash, scooping up great
handfuls of golden treasure and giggling with mad
delight as they crammed it into their bags. They
filled their pockets too, slipped bracelets on their
wrists and rings on every finger.

Then there
was a sound.

Everyone froze.

'What was that?' said Shifty, cocking an ear to listen.

'It was nothing,' said Crusher, shoving a third tiara onto his bald, stubbly head. 'You've got the jitters, that's all.'

Shifty listened for a moment more, but hearing nothing, started digging out rubies from a jewelled box with the tip of his knife.

They froze again.

'OK, tell me you didn't hear it that time?' said Shifty, his voice going a bit squeaky.

'I think it came from . . . that,' said Jelly, staring wide-eyed at the golden skull.

'It was the wind, you gibbering goons!' snapped Pickering. 'Just the wind! Now get on with it!'

Ben was backing away as far as the leash would let him.

It's the **THIRD SIGN!** The haunting moans! **THE MUMMY'S COMING!** You're mad, Pickering! You're going to get us all **SHRIVELLED UP!**

'Er, perhaps we should scarper, eh boss?' said Shifty, gingerly stepping away. 'We've got plenty of loot.'

'You stay where you are!' hissed Pickering viciously. 'We're not going anywhere without that crown!'

He turned and stepped towards the golden skull, his eyes fixed on the Mummy's Crown and its enormous glittering diamond.

He reached for it. His quivering fingertips stretched out, just inches away. The room fell deathly quiet as everyone held their breath.

192

In a flash, the skull shot upwards with a booming moan and towered over Pickering. Bony hands stretched out from beneath billowing robes, and light blazed from the skull's hollow eyes.

Pickering shrieked. He fell backwards, letting Ben's leash slip from his fingers. Pickering then scrabbled to get away, bumped into Ben and knocked him, stumbling, into the Mummy's clutches!

'It's got him!' shouted Shifty. 'It's got Pole!'

The Mummy's cloak swirled round Ben and he vanished.

There was a muffled scream and then silence.

The Midnight Mob watched in horror as the Mummy's cloak swept slowly open.

There on the floor lay Ben.

He was shrivelled to a nub!

That was it! Jelly, Dodge, Shifty and Crusher bolted shrieking for the door, flapping about like wet hens, throwing off their jewellery and emptying their pockets as they went.

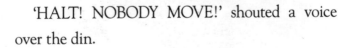

'HALT! NOBODY MOVE!' shouted a voice over the din.

CHAPTER FOURTEEN

Mrs Pole stood framed in the doorway, shielding her eyes from the dazzling torchlight.

The gang of stubby little men threw themselves at her feet, trembling like jellies.

'SAVE US, MISSUS!' they begged and pleaded.

'IT'S THE MUMMY'S CURSE!' they shouted over each other.

'We didn't *mean* to steal all the stuff!'

'Just get us out of here before we gets shrivelled by the Mummy!'

'A nice jail cell – lock us up nice and safe! PLEASE, MISSUS!'

Without a moment's hesitation, Mrs Pole hoisted the men onto their feet, dragged them out into the corridor like sacks of porridge, and locked them in a broom cupboard.

With the peculiar little men safely tucked away, she strode back into the Treasure Chamber.

It was a mess. Treasure was strewn all over the floor. The rest of it was packed in big black bags.

The golden skull was back on display, as still as the grave.

205

'You were brilliant!' said Ben, emerging from the dark. Mrs Pole goggled. 'What are YOU doing here? Are you OK? Who ARE those men and what's all this about shrivelling their mummy? Come on, let's get out of here! We've got to call the police!'

'There's no hurry, Mrs P,' said Coo, strolling up to her as cool as a freshly refrigerated cucumber.

'COO! Is that you?' Mrs Pole squinted, looking more confused than ever. 'What on earth are you two DOING here? And why are you dressed like that? What's with the hairy outfit? I think you two have got some explaining to do, don't you?'

'Outfit? Oh yeah, my *outfit*,' said Coo, nudging Ben and winking. 'Well, it's a long story, Mrs P, but in a nutshell, me and Ben here had to play a few tricks to save the treasure from the Midnight Mob.'

A pair of hands shot out from the shadows and snatched Ben by the collar.

I KNEW IT!

Pickering!

Ben gurgled, half choking.

'Yes, POLE! SURPRISE!' screamed Pickering, backing away and dragging Ben along with him.

'I knew it was all a fake! I TOLD YOU, DIDN'T I? It takes more than a schoolboy and a . . . a . . .' He glanced at Coo. 'A . . . well . . . a hairy one of THOSE to get the better of Percy Pickering! The TREASURE is MINE!' he bellowed, his one eye swivelling madly about in his head as he spoke. 'MINE!'

'Stay where you are, Pickering,' commanded Mrs Pole. 'Let Ben go!'

'Oh no,' said Pickering, tightening his grip. 'Ben is coming with me. He's going to help me carry all this loot. Any tricks and he'll WISH he'd been shrivelled by the Mummy compared to what I'll do to him, so no funny business, got it?'

But Mrs Pole and Coo weren't looking at Pickering any more. They were staring past him, at one of the statues.

'Coo, love?' said Mrs Pole, her voice a little shaky.

If it was YOU doing all the tricks, and you're standing <u>here</u>, then HOW IS THAT STATUE MOVING?

'Ha! Nice try!' scoffed Pickering, turning to glance behind him.

I'm not falling for THAT old...

Pickering shrieked like a startled weasel, let go of Ben, and sprinted for the door.

'He's escaping!' shouted Ben.

'Not for long,' said Coo, flipping a gold cup up off the floor with her foot and catching it in her hand. She threw it hard and fast. It hit Pickering *THUNK* on the back of the head and knocked him out cold.

THUNK!

Ben turned and stared wide-eyed at the statue.

It stepped forwards, looming out of the shadows.

CHAPTER FIFTEEN

The next morning was bright and crisp. Autumn sun streamed in through the windows of Mr and Mrs Pole's little house.

DING DONG!

'I'll get it,' yelled Ben. 'That'll be Coo.'

'Morning, Pole!' said Coo, standing on the doorstep with Herbert by her side wagging his rump cheerfully.

'No beard then?' said Ben, looking Coo up and down. 'Worried about startling Mum and Dad, eh?'

'I don't think they're quite ready for it yet, do you?' she said, stroking her smooth cheeks. 'Maybe next time.'

'Come on in. We've got a guest,' said Ben, hanging Coo's crown on the hallstand as Mr Pole strode past carrying a teapot and a plate stacked with crumpets.

'Coo! Herbert!' he boomed cheerfully. 'It sounds like you all had a busy night! Crooks, police, arrests! I expect you could do with a crumpet, eh? Come on through.'

217

In the living room, sipping tea, were Mrs Pole and the *living statue*.

'Hello, Coo,' said Mrs Pole. She turned to her guest. 'You've met Chief Umpopo.'

'Hello again, chief!' said Coo.

Chief Umpopo smiled one of those smiles that show ALL your teeth. He stood up and put his hands on Coo's shoulders.

'Hello, my friend,' he said. 'I came to thank you all for saving the Mummy's Gold. Your quick wits and your courage will for ever be remembered by the Blue-foots.'

'Happy to help, chief.' Coo grinned.

'Help yourself to some breakfast, love,' said Mrs Pole warmly. 'We were just talking about all the excitement last night.'

'Oh, thanks!' said Coo, dropping onto the sofa beside Ben, grabbing a cup of hot tea and deftly stabbing three crumpets with the tip of her spear.

'You didn't half give me a fright last night, Mr Umpopo,' said Mrs Pole, smiling. 'I really thought you were a statue come to life!'

'I'm awfully sorry!' said Chief Umpopo. 'It all happened so fast!'

221

'So how come you were there in the first place?' asked Mr Pole, sitting back in his armchair and offering Herbert a bite of his buttered crumpet.

'Well, it's like this,' explained the chief. 'I was over the moon to hear that our Mummy's Gold had been recovered. And to be invited along to the exhibition, before taking the treasure home to my tribe, was just too exciting! I couldn't wait to see it, so I popped along to the museum yesterday for a peek.'

'And you got locked in?' said Mrs Pole.

'Yes! What a nincompoop!' The chief blushed. 'I got carried away and didn't realize it was closing time. I settled in for the night, feeling terribly embarrassed. But it got quite chilly so I slipped on one of the tribal costumes.'

'And when the Midnight Mob burst in?' asked Mr Pole, wiping butter off his beard.

'Gracious! It was quite a shock, I can tell you!' chuckled the chief. 'I just stood still. As still as a . . . well, a statue! It was pretty dark in there. No one noticed me.'

'Blimey!'

'And then all of a sudden, there was the Mummy, and well, you know the rest.'

'Speaking of which, now you're here, Coo,' said Mrs Pole, 'please tell us, *how* did you do it? You know, bringing the Mummy's Curse to life?'

Coo smiled her sidelong smile. 'Well, it all began when Ben turned up yesterday, babbling something about Pickering and a gold coin . . .' said Coo.

Everyone leaned forward to listen, quietly munching their breakfast while Coo explained how she and Ben had discovered the truth about the Midnight Mob, found their hideout and overheard their plans to steal the Mummy's Gold.

'So they tricked their way into schools in disguise, then wangled field trips to check out the museums and plan their robberies?' said Mr Pole with a hint of admiration.

Pretty clever, that.

'They had *me* fooled,' said Ben. 'Right up until I saw them in the hideout. Not Coo though. She saw right through them. The next thing I know she whispers some instructions, winks at me and pushes me off the ledge, *right* into Pickering's hands!'

'Ha! You should've seen your face!' chuckled Coo, tossing her last bite of crumpet into the air and catching it in her mouth.

'So, anyway,' Coo continued, 'I hid until the coast was clear then snuck back and listened to Ben doing his bit and telling Pickering and his mob about the curse.'

'You were brilliant, Ben, acting scared and telling them all that CURSE rubbish! I almost believed you myself!' Coo paused to slurp her tea. 'After that, I picked up a few bits and bobs from the tree house and slipped into the museum before closing.'

CITY
MUSEUM

'Yes, yes, but come on, HOW did you do the curses?' said Mr Pole. 'I mean, it *was* you, wasn't it? The gold isn't *really* cursed, is it?'

'I don't know about the real Mummy's Curse, Mr P.' Coo grinned. 'But the Ben Pole version certainly had a little help from me.'

She pulled some drawings from her bag and spread them out on the table.

'Look, these plans will help explain. OK, so Ben told the Midnight Mob that there were three signs to show you'd been cursed, and he made sure they noticed them all. I just had to bring them to life.'

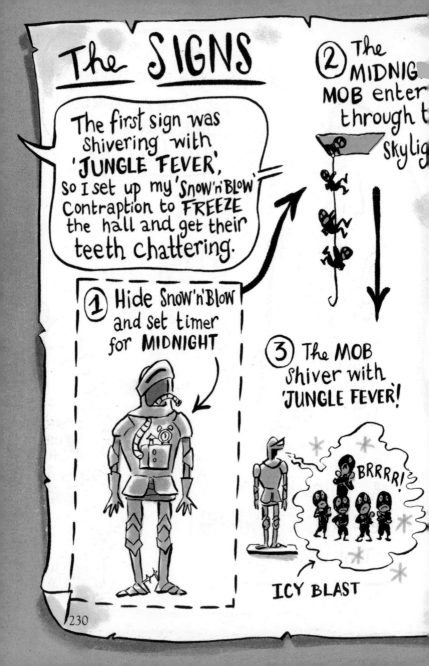

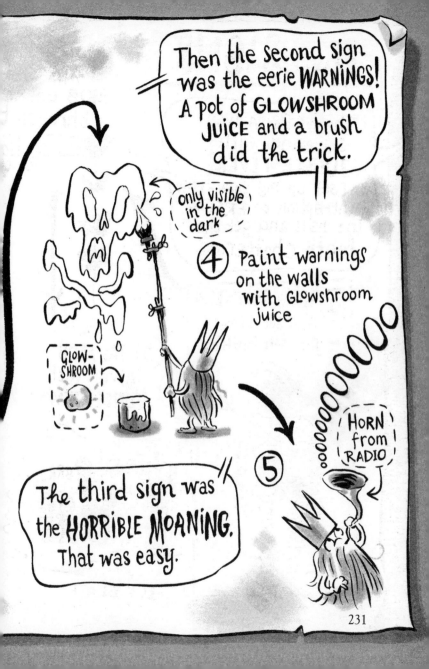

Then to finish them off I thought it was time for the MUMMY to appear and shrivel Ben.
The MUMMY'S CURSE
part one
PLAN:
Crown
Golden Skull
Plinth
1
cloth
1 Set up Mummy
2 Bring Mummy to life
3 TERRIFY the MIDNIGHT MOB and send them CRACKERS!

And THIS is how I did it!

The MUMMY'S CURSE part two

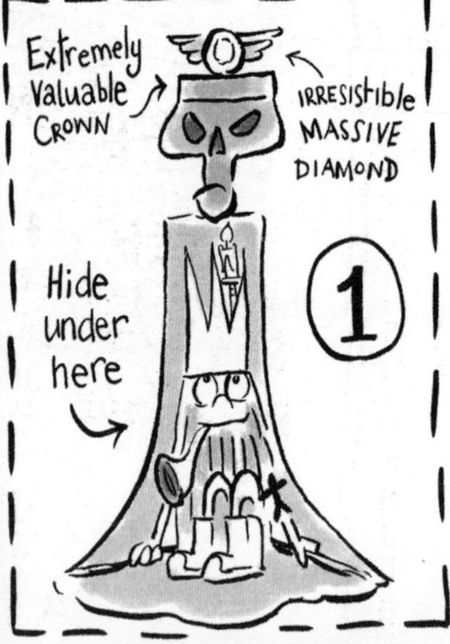

The Solution:

1. Hide under the plinth and wait for the MIDNIGHT MOB
2. use bits and bobs from my TREEHOUSE to bring the MUMMY to life!

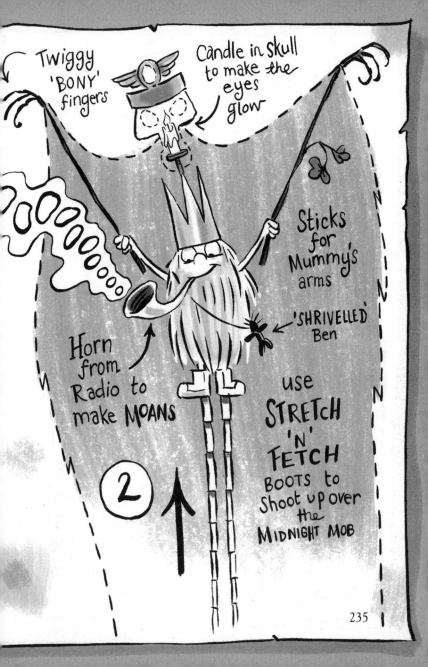

235

'Ha! Well knock me down with a lemon jelly! You've done it again, Coo! AMAZING!' said Mr Pole, patting her heartily on the back. 'Absolutely marvellous! Um, so those boots in your bag over there, are they the Stretch'n'Fetch ones?' he added, getting up and going for a closer look.

'The tribe will be very proud of you, Coo,' said the chief warmly.

'I know I am,' said Mrs Pole, leaning in to hug Coo and Ben and rub Herbert's chops. 'I'm proud of you all. And I must say, Coo, that hairy outfit was fantastic! A little extra touch to blend in with the exhibits, was it?' she added. 'It's VERY lifelike.'

Coo glanced at Ben. 'Yes, you could say that, Mrs P,' she said, smiling. '*Very* lifelike.'

'Anyway,' said Mrs Pole, getting to her feet, 'we had better go. It's the Mummy's Gold grand opening tonight, and there's lots of clearing up to do. Coo, we'll drop you and Ben off at the woods on the way, OK?'

'Coo, Ben, I trust we will see you tonight?' said Chief Umpopo.

'We'll be there,' said Coo, shaking his hand.

'WOOOOOOOOOAAAH! OOooopsadaisy!' Mr Pole's voice drifted in from outside.

'Oh no!' said Ben, rushing to the window. 'Dad's got hold of your Stretch'n'Fetch boots!'

'DAD! CLICK YOUR HEELS!' yelled Ben through cupped hands.

'What was that, lad?' said Mr Pole as he wobbled off down the garden and tripped over the shed. '*Lick more eels?* How's THAT going to help?'

Back at the tree house, Ben and Herbert lay stretched out on an enormous hammock in the autumn sunshine enjoying the peace and quiet. Mr Pole had been rescued, and had whizzed off to the museum with the others.

Ben chuckled when Coo strolled out from her hut to join them, a cup in each hand. She was back to normal. Her fresh thick beard blew gently in the breeze.

'I'll never know how you grow that thing so fast,' he said, reaching for the ginger beer she offered him.

'Practice,' she replied.

'So, Coo, how come you know Chief Umpopo?' asked Ben, propping himself up on one elbow to look at her. 'I've been wondering about that since yesterday.'

'Oh that,' said Coo hopping onto the hammock. 'I get around, you know. I'm sure I told you, there was this one time I was floating down the Amazon river in a biscuit tin . . .'

Herbert rolled onto his back for Coo to scratch his belly while she spoke, and by the time her story was over, he was snoring gently.

'Not a bad night's work last night, eh, Ben?' she said. 'We saved the Mummy's Gold for Chief Umpopo, your mum will get promoted for bravery, and my woods are crook-free again.'

'Yeah. Not bad at all. Oh, did you hear?' Ben sat up. 'Apparently, there's been a mix up. Pickering and his Midnight Mob have been sent to do hard time at the Peril Beach Correctional Institute for Unruly Girls! Tougher than any prison!'

'Ha! Serves them right, after what they did to your poor Mr Travis,' said Coo.

'How come you knew they were men, back in the hideout?' Ben wondered. 'They had me fooled all along.'

'Oh, there were a few signs, if you knew where to look,' said Coo.

'But mostly it was just one thing,' she added.

'Yes? What?'

'They were TOO girly,' said Coo, idly picking a dead leaf from her beard. 'No girl is THAT girly!'

Ben giggled, lay back down and watched the yellowing leaves above blow in the breeze.

'What *was* that thing made from?' he said. 'That shrivelled version of me? It looked horrible! It scared me half to death.'

'Oh, that?' Coo grinned. 'Yeah, pretty ugly, wasn't it? Well I suppose you have your dad to thank for that.'

SHRIVELLED BEN

Button eyes

Burnt sausages

Wombat hair

'No!'

'Yup!'

'His SAUSAGES?'

'Ha! You've got it!' said Coo. 'They were the most mummified things I could find!'

'Brilliant!' said Ben, dabbing his eyes. 'Just brilliant!'

Coo grabbed Herbert and got up, leaving Ben sprawled in the hammock.

'Are you off somewhere?' asked Ben, looking up and shielding his eyes from the sun.

'No,' said Coo. 'This just seems like a good time.'

Ben sat up. 'For what?'

Coo had one of *those* looks. And she was standing suspiciously close to a big lever.

'It's my latest thing,' said Coo with a grin.

I call it the SKY-HIGH HAMMOCK!

'Really?'

'Yes.'

'Now?'

'Why not?'

Ben couldn't think of a good enough reason. It was just another day in Coo's woods. He smiled.

'Go on then.'

'Trust me.' Coo winked . . .

ACKNOWLEDGEMENTS

I'd like to thank everyone at David Fickling Books for their boundless enthusiasm during the making of this book. Thank you Rosie and Bella for your guidance and encouragement, and Alison for helping to bring it all together so beautifully.

I would also like to thank:

Tamlyn and Caroline at Arena Illustration for their continuing friendship and all their hard work on my behalf,

My wonderful family and friends for their support,

And especially my wife Zoë, and my daughter, Mary, for their love and patience.

A.S.

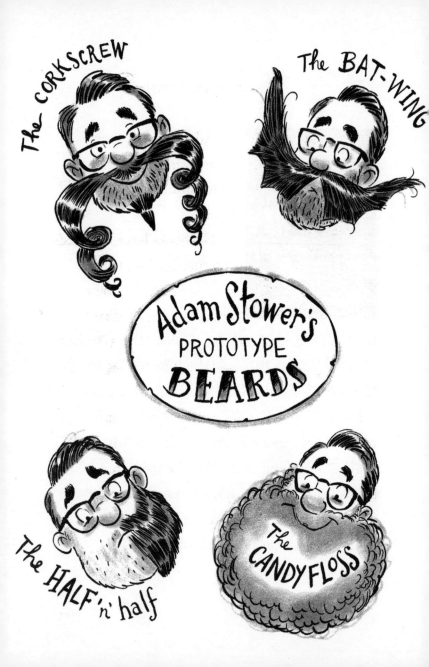

About Adam Stower

Author photo: Paul Winter

Adam Stower is an award-winning author and illustrator of children's books.

His books have received international acclaim, winning prizes at home and abroad, including the Red House Book Award for *Bottom's Up!* (Author – Jeanne Willis) 2010 and the Wanda Gag Read-Aloud Book Award (US) for *Silly Doggy!* 2013.

Much of *King Coo* was inspired by Adam's memories of playing in the woods with his brother, Matt, and of the time he spent at a 462-year-old boarding school in north Norfolk.

Adam lives in Brighton, with his wife, his daughter and a cat called Murray.

PERFECT PLANTS